TALES OF THE

FIVE *Enchanted* MERMAIDS™

# You Can Do it!

Lois Petren

Other books by Lois Petren:

Lulu and Lainey ... a French Yarn
Lulu and Lainey ... a Christmas Yarn
Lulu and Lainey ... the Lucky Day
Lulu and Lainey ... at the Farm
Lulu and Lainey ... Color with Us
Lulu and Lainey --- 12 Days of Christmas
Tales of the Five Enchanted Mermaids
    - Coloring and Activity Book

Paperback ISBN-13: 978-0-9998099-6-9

Otto was mad – and sad.

Otto was a little octopus in the magical land of Atargatis who spent his days at Miss Molly's School. One day he wanted to make a castle with plastic blocks but didn't know how.

MISS MOLLY'S SCHOOL

He was so mad that he turned red, yelled at his friends and threw the blocks into the sand. No one wanted to play with him and that made him sad.

As he went home he saw the Five Enchanted Mermaids swimming along.

Everyone loved the mermaids because they were so kind and helpful. They had magical skills that helped the children learn about their world.

The mermaids saw that he was unhappy and stopped to give him a hug. He told them why he was upset and they all said "We can help!"

This helped him get calm and he turned back to his usual color.

First he turned to Anna, who knows all about how to be kind and patient.

Anna said, "It will be easier to find a solution if we are kind and patient with ourselves. Can you think of some ideas to do that?"

He thought about it and came up with some ideas.

Then he asked Sofia if she could help.
Sofia helps kids learn to be honest and
truthful.

Sofia said "Sometimes we're afraid of something, but we don't understand why. If you know what scares you then you can fix it."

Otto thought for a bit and realized what he was upset about.

Jenny, who is very confident, stepped up to speak. She wanted to help because she knows how to help kids like themselves.

"Otto," she said with a wink and a smile,
"let's think of some ways to help you like
yourself more."

Then Emily, the bravest of the mermaids, came forward to tell Otto about ways he can be brave and overcome his fears.

"Otto, if you're afraid to learn something new it's hard to do things you want to do. So, if you learn how to use the blocks you can play with your friends again. I want to help you do that."

Here are some ideas they thought of.

Zari waited patiently for the others to finish so Otto could hear from them first. Now it was her turn. Zari knew a lot about how to be independent.

"Being independent means that you're ready to do something on your own.

Sometimes you know you're ready but other times you need to find the courage

The next day Otto went back to school and:

- sat with his legs crossed and said kind words to himself

- decided it was OK to make a mistake

- thought about the things he was good at doing – like opening jars

- pictured himself as a brave knight on a quest

- worked with the plastic blocks until he found a way to link them together

He was able to make a little castle. His friends were so happy that they cheered for him!

He held up the castle he made, let out a cheer, and said "I can do it!"

Miss Molly's School

To stay informed about new books, party sets, and other items, join our community at https://www.fiveenchantedmermaids.com/ and our Facebook page at https://www.facebook.com/fiveenchantedmermaids/.